The Rescue Princesses

The Magic Rings

More amazing animal adventures!

The Secret Promise

The Wishing Pearl

The Moonlight Mystery

The Stolen Crystals

The Snow Jewel

The Rescue Princesses

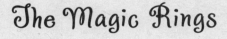

The Magic Rings

💙 PAULA HARRISON 💙

Scholastic Inc.

For Jennie, the best sister in the kingdom

No part of this publication may be reproduced, stored in a retrieval system, or transmitted in any form or by any means, electronic, mechanical, photocopying, recording, or otherwise, without written permission of the publisher. For information regarding permission, write to Nosy Crow Ltd., The Crow's Nest, 10a Lant Street, London, SE1 1QR, UK.

ISBN 978-0-545-50918-3

12 11 10 9 8 7   15 16 17 18/0

First printing, October 2013

CHAPTER ONE

Royal Sisters

Princess Lottie spun around the bedroom as fast as she could, her red dress swirling. She turned around and around, until she got so dizzy that she collapsed, laughing, on top of the velvet blanket.

"Stop it, Lottie!" exclaimed Princess Emily. "You're squishing all the things I was just about to pack."

Lottie yanked a pile of creased clothes out from underneath her. Then she bounced up to peer into the enormous suitcase that lay next to her on the bed. It was full of dresses, tiaras, and a hairbrush with a diamond-studded handle.

"You can't fit anything else in there, anyway," she said bluntly. "How much stuff do you need at your Royal School Thingy?"

"The Royal Academy for Princesses," Emily corrected her. "You have to have clothes for lessons, clothes for parties, clothes for ceremonies, and much more. I'll need all of these. There'll be so many special occasions to go to."

Lottie yawned. "Poor you! It sounds boring. I hope I don't have to go when I'm older."

Emily frowned. "It's important for every princess to learn how to fulfill her duties, you know."

Lottie chuckled. "You sound just like Mom." She tried out a fancy accent.

"*A princess must perform splendid and magnificent duties, like spinning around as many times as she can before she falls over!*" She leapt off the bed and started twirling again.

"Lottie! Stop it!" groaned Emily. Then she sat down on her bed and sighed.

Lottie stopped spinning and landed beside her sister, making the bed wobble.

"I guess I do sound a little bit like Mom," said Emily. "I still like having fun, though, and I'm going to be seeing all my friends at the academy."

"I'll miss you!" Lottie gave her sister a quick hug. "Even though you like to whine!"

"I'll miss you, too." Emily grinned. "Even though you squish my clothes!"

Lottie looked at the mirror on the wall, where their reflections sat side by side.

Everybody always said it was easy

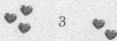

to tell that they were sisters, mainly because their hair was exactly the same red color, like a flame. But while Emily's hair hung over her shoulders in loose waves, Lottie's was clustered into tight curls. Their eyes were different, too. Lottie's were a bright sparkling green while Emily's were a gentler hazel.

Lottie had always wished she was the older one. But now she was glad she wasn't leaving for school. Emily said the academy would be exciting, but Lottie wasn't so sure.

"If you've left any tiaras behind, can I borrow them while you're gone?" asked Lottie, itching to look in Emily's closet.

But Emily wasn't listening. She gazed thoughtfully at her sister, twisting a lock of red hair around her finger.

"Why are you staring at me like that?"

asked Lottie. "I promise I'll put the tiaras back. I know I broke that silver one. But that was a long time ago."

"There's something I need to tell you," said Emily slowly. "You know that time you heard me and my friends talking about being Rescue Princesses when we were staying in Northernland?"

"Yes, it sounded like a really good game." Lottie pouted. "And I think you should have let me join from the start."

"It wasn't a game at all," said Emily. "I was just worried that you were too little to know about it."

"I am NOT little!" Lottie burst out.

"I guess not." Emily smiled. "Now that you've had your birthday, you're the same age as I was when I first became a Rescue Princess! Jaminta, Clarabel, and Lulu have all sent me their magic rings, so I can explain that part, too."

"What?" Lottie nearly bounced off the bed. "What magic rings?"

"Hold on! I need to tell you everything from the beginning," said Emily. "Just listen! And try not to interrupt!"

Lottie frowned, but then decided to be patient. After all, she wanted to know what Emily was going to say. "Tell me, then. What's this Rescue Princesses thing all about?"

Emily lowered her voice to a whisper. "Do you remember two years ago, when I went to Mistberg Castle for the Grand Ball? And you didn't come because you had chicken pox?"

Lottie nodded.

"Well, that's when I met the other princesses and we had our first adventure, rescuing the Mistberg deer from metal traps that had been left in the forest. It was really exciting, doing it all

by ourselves! After that we promised each other that we would always rescue any animals in danger. And we have, lots of times!"

Emily fumbled in her pocket and pulled out four rings, each with a beautiful heart-shaped jewel in the center. The red, blue, green, and yellow gems glittered in the palm of her hand.

"Your ruby ring!" said Lottie, picking up the glowing red jewel. "You always wear this one. Aren't you taking it with you to the academy?"

"No, I'm not, and you have to listen to me," said Emily urgently. "They'll send someone along for my suitcase in a minute and then I'll have to go."

"OK, I'm listening." Lottie fixed her green eyes on Emily.

"The four of us became the Rescue Princesses, and we've rescued lots of different animals all over the world. Now it's your turn. I can't rescue animals when I'm at school. You'll have to do it. Find some other princesses, ones that you trust, and do it together." Emily gazed at her sister earnestly. "You'll have to do what we did. Train hard. Learn to climb, swing, and balance. Practice ninja moves. . . ."

"Ninja moves?!" Lottie's eyes grew even wider.

"Yes! Ally taught them to us. You know that she used to be an undercover agent before she came to work here. She's the only other person who knows about the Rescue Princesses."

"You really learned ninja moves?"

"Yes! And we used jewels with special powers. We had a lot of them, but these rings are the only ones I can give you right now." Emily dropped the other three rings into Lottie's hand. "This green jewel is an emerald, the blue one is a sapphire, and the yellow one is a topaz. We used them to contact each other when we were far apart. You have to press the jewel and speak into it when it lights up."

Just then, footsteps sounded in the hallway and the door handle swung slowly down. Lottie quickly hid the four rings behind her back and the girls held their breath. Ally, their maid, came in, carrying a pile of folded towels. The girls breathed a sigh of relief.

"Are you almost ready, Princess Emily?" asked Ally. "Your carriage is waiting downstairs."

Emily closed her suitcase and zipped it up. "I'm ready now!" She turned to Lottie. "You will be careful, right? Sometimes you rush off and do things without thinking."

Lottie made a face. "I'll be careful!"

Emily smiled. "Good-bye, then! Look after those rings!"

"Bye, Emily!" Lottie gave her sister one last hug, and then Emily was gone.

Lottie watched from the upstairs window as Emily's carriage rolled away. She held the four rings tightly, with a fluttering feeling in her stomach. Now it was her turn to be a Rescue Princess. She would seek out animals in danger and save them with fearless acrobatics and cunning ninja moves.

Emily had told her to be careful. But that was just her worrying about nothing. Lottie had always been able to look after herself. She'd probably make a better Rescue Princess than her sister, anyway!

CHAPTER TWO

The Royal Dance Festival

Lottie leaned forward to look out the tiny, square airplane window. A whole week had passed since Emily had left for school. A whole week since she'd told Lottie about the Rescue Princesses! In that week Lottie had only managed to rescue one creature from danger, and that had been a bumblebee buzzing around her bedroom. She'd just opened the window and let the bee fly away. It hadn't been very exciting.

But this place would be different. Down below, she could see rolling hills dotted with small patches of woodland. Surely there'd be lots of animals to rescue there, maybe rabbits or badgers, or even a brown bear?

She was going to the kingdom of Peronia with her mom, dad, and Ally, to attend the Royal Dance Festival. Lots of royal families would be there. They would spend several days dancing and hold a grand performance on the final day.

Her dad smiled at her across the aisle of the plane. "We'll be there soon, Lottie. Did you remember to pack all your dancing shoes?"

Lottie nodded. "Ballet shoes, tap shoes, and jazz shoes."

"Ah, if only I was young again! Your mom and I really knew how to rock and roll," said the king of Middingland dreamily. "Our favorite dance was called the jitterbug!"

Lottie grinned at the thought of her mom and dad bopping around in their crowns and robes. She loved dancing and couldn't wait for the festival. But she wasn't just going there to dance. She was searching for girls who loved animals and adventure to join the Rescue Princesses. She unzipped her shoulder bag and peeked at the four jeweled rings lying safe inside. She loved the ruby ring the most, which was the one that Emily used to wear.

Checking to be sure that no one was looking, she picked up the ring and pressed the ruby firmly. Nothing happened. She sighed and put it back in the bag again. She had tried the ring several times now, but it never lit up the way that Emily had told her it did.

Maybe Ally would know why it wasn't working.

The airplane landed on the runway. They all climbed down the steps and got into a polished silver car that would take them the short distance to the Peronian Palace. Lottie stared out of the window as hedges flashed past, searching for signs of birds or animals that might need help.

After a while, a row of tall gray towers rose above the hedges. They turned a corner and the whole palace came into view. It was a magnificent place with an enormous arched front door. Lottie counted twenty-two turrets along the roof. It was certainly one of the grandest palaces she'd ever seen.

"Mom?" Lottie asked suddenly. "There will be other princesses at this dance festival, won't there?"

"Of course," said her mom briskly. "There will be plenty of princesses, and princes, too. Just remember that you are from the royal family of Middingland, and must always behave with the utmost politeness."

Lottie nodded, her face lighting up. Plenty of princesses. That would mean plenty of potential *Rescue* Princesses!

They rolled slowly up the gravel driveway, passing a boy with muddy boots leading a beautiful sandy-colored horse. The boy frowned at them, but Lottie was too busy looking at the horse to pay much attention. She loved horses and spent hours grooming them in the palace stables back home in Middingland. This horse had lovely chocolate-brown eyes and had been brushed until its coat shone.

The car stopped at the front door just as a lady with a huge wide-brimmed hat

came bustling out to meet them. Lottie couldn't help staring at her hat. It was lime green and covered with plastic purple grapes.

"Here's Queen Sofia of Peronia! Please remember to curtsy, Lottie," said her mom.

"How wonderful to see you," boomed Queen Sofia.

Lottie climbed out of the car and performed her best curtsy. She knew it was a little wobbly, but at least she didn't fall over.

"Thank you so much for inviting us to visit," said the queen of Middingland.

"Not at all! Now let me show you where you're staying." Queen Sofia led them into the palace, her lime-green hat bobbing as she walked.

The palace was full of royal visitors. Orange lamps glowed on the walls, lighting up huge paintings of soldiers galloping on horses. Queen Sofia led them up a grand staircase and down many hallways, until she suddenly stopped.

"These are your rooms, my dears." The queen patted Lottie on the head. "I hope we'll see some splendid dancing from you. You look like just the kind of princess to treat us to a bouncy jig!"

Lottie grimaced, but remembered just in time that she was supposed to be polite. "Umm, thank you," she said.

"Wonderful! Now, the opening ceremony starts in half an hour," said the queen. "I'll go and let you get settled in."

While her mom and dad thanked Queen Sofia, Lottie pushed open the door to her room. It had a thick red carpet and a large cuckoo clock hanging on the wall. Lottie ran straight to the window and pulled up the sash. The walls around the palace grounds were high, but she could still see the countryside beyond. A cool breeze played with the curtains and birdsong drifted over from nearby trees.

There was a knock on the door. Ally came in with her suitcase and set it down on the bed. "This is such a beautiful country," she said, seeing Lottie at the window.

Lottie smiled. "There must be lots of animals outside those walls, and maybe some of them need help! I can't wait to go and explore."

Ally frowned a little. "I know Emily asked you to look out for animals in trouble, but your parents won't like it if you leave the dance festival too often." She opened the case and began unpacking dance skirts and ballet shoes.

"That's why I have to learn more ninja moves. That way I can sneak out without anyone seeing me." Lottie's eyes gleamed.

Ally smiled. "I think you'll be very good at ninja moves once you've had a little more practice."

"Oh! I just remembered. I have something important to ask you." Lottie unzipped her bag and poured the jeweled rings out into her hand. "These rings aren't working. Look, when I press them nothing happens." She pressed the ruby, sapphire, emerald, and yellow topaz. Although they sparkled beautifully, none of them lit up or did anything exciting.

"That's odd," said Ally, looking closer. "I don't know much about Emily's special jewels. They have a magic all their own."

Lottie tucked them away in her bag. "There must be a way to get them to work. I'll just have to keep trying."

"You will be careful, won't you, Princess Lottie?" asked Ally. "I don't want you rushing into something and getting hurt."

"Oh, don't worry!" Lottie said airily. "I won't get hurt. I never do!"

There was a knock at the door and her mom called her name.

"I'm almost ready!" Lottie grabbed her best party dress from the suitcase and yanked it on. It was a deep crimson red and covered with lots of sparkly sequins. She picked up her favorite tiara, a zigzag one decorated with rubies, and rammed it on top of her curls. Then, shooting Ally a quick grin, she raced from the room, letting the door swing out wide behind her.

CHAPTER THREE

Lottie's Dance Escape

The opening ceremony was held in a hall with a high ceiling. The walls were covered in spears and shields made from polished metal. Kings and queens clustered around, sipping tea and nibbling cake. Lottie followed her parents to the front of the hall and managed another curtsy to Queen Sofia, who was still wearing her lime-green hat.

While her parents chatted, Lottie scanned the room excitedly. This was her first chance to look for princesses to join her — princesses who wanted adventure.

She spotted one girl standing in a corner, wearing a long turquoise dress. The girl had brown eyes and straight black hair that fell down to her waist. Lottie stared at her for a moment, but the other girl looked shy and turned away. She seemed nice, Lottie thought, but maybe she was too nervous to be a Rescue Princess.

Then she noticed a second princess. This girl had dark hair that hung in loose curls, a floaty yellow dress, and eyes that sparkled with excitement. She looked much more adventurous. But just then she bumped into a table, sending a pile of cherry cakes cascading to the floor. People ran forward, hurrying to pick them up. Lottie frowned; would a princess who was so clumsy really be good at animal rescues?

She scanned the room one more time. Her eyes stopped on a princess in a dark blue dress with short blonde hair. But this girl was arguing with the boy standing next to her, pointing her finger straight at him and scowling. Lottie raised her eyebrows in surprise. She hadn't realized it would be so tricky finding princesses that seemed just right.

Just at that moment, Queen Sofia clapped her hands. "Your Royal Highnesses! Welcome to Peronia, and here's to a wonderful Dance Festival. Now we'll finish the opening ceremony with our first dance!"

Lottie's eyes sparkled. A dance! What would it be?

"Let's perform the Bobbing Dance,"

continued the queen. "Please form two straight lines."

Lottie stifled a groan. The Bobbing Dance was the one that her mom had made her practice before they left home. It was a long dance set to dull, slow music. All you did was bob up and down and curtsy to the other dancers. It made her yawn every time she practiced it. Why couldn't they choose something more exciting?

The kings, queens, princes, and princesses arranged themselves into two long lines facing each other. Lottie stood at one end, near an open door that led out into a garden. Through the doorway, she could see green lawns and large flower beds full of tulips. She gazed out at them longingly.

A woman started to play a tune on the piano. The royal dancers began to bob up and down, and Lottie reluctantly did the same. But the hall was small for so many dancers. Two kings bumped into each other. Then the princess in the yellow dress stepped on Queen Sofia's toe, making her hop around holding on to her foot. The music stopped for a moment.

"Spread out please, Your Majesties! We don't want anyone to get hurt," called the woman at the piano. "Is everyone ready for the final part of the dance?"

Lottie ended up moving next to the garden door as everyone tried to spread out. She could see more and more of the garden now. Beyond the tulips was a long row of fountains, and beyond that was a field with a sandy-colored horse. Maybe it was the same one she'd seen when they arrived. She looked closer. The horse stood next to the fence, staring at the palace, as if it wanted to gallop across the garden and dance with them.

Lottie giggled at the thought of the horse joining in. She wished she could run over and pet it.

She turned around to look at the dancing kings and queens. Maybe she could? No one had spotted that she was standing right by the door. If she sneaked out before the music stopped, then no one would notice her leaving. But she would have to be quick!

Her heart began to thump. She shot one last look at the dancing royals, and then dived through the open doorway. The bright sunlight was dazzling, and her crimson dress billowed out around her legs as she ran. She passed the flower beds, where patches of red and gold tulips swayed in the breeze. She passed the row of carved fountains, where arching jets of water scattered spray over her head. The music from the hall faded behind her.

She stopped at the fence and tried to catch her breath. But the horse wasn't there anymore. It was trotting away across the field.

"Come back!" called Lottie, but the horse tossed its mane and continued trotting.

Lottie ran beside the fence until she got to a gate. The horse slowed down as it reached a long brick building with a low roof. Lottie counted seven more horses inside, their heads looking out over their stable doors. Opening the gate, she walked across the rough grass toward the building. She smiled as she walked inside. It was dark in here and it smelled of hay. It reminded her of the stables at home.

The sandy-colored horse stopped and turned back to nuzzle her shoulder.

"You're very friendly! What's your name?" asked Lottie softly, stroking the animal's nose.

"She's called Honey," said a voice from the shadows. "And *you* shouldn't be here."

Lottie spun around to see a boy leaning on the end of a broom and frowning at her. She recognized him as the boy she'd seen earlier, leading the horse up the drive. He looked even grumpier than before. But Lottie didn't mind that.

"It's OK! I'm sure the grown-ups won't notice that I'm gone." She grinned widely at him. "This is a great stable. How many horses are here?"

The boy's frown disappeared. "We have twenty-five of them. Actually twenty-six now, because one was born two weeks ago."

"A foal!" cried Lottie. "Where is it?"

The boy jerked a thumb over his shoulder. "Her name is Twinkle."

Lottie hurried up to the stall and peered over. A mare and her foal were lying down together on the hay. The foal was chocolaty brown with a white star on her forehead. She looked at Lottie and her soft ears twitched.

"She's lovely!" breathed Lottie. "She's the most beautiful foal I've ever seen!"

CHAPTER FOUR

A Foal Named Twinkle

"I'm Lottie, by the way," said Lottie.

"You mean, Princess Lottie," said the boy, looking at her tiara and her crimson dress, which now had bits of straw sticking to it. "And I'm Peter."

"Why don't I give you a hand grooming the horses? I'm sure you could use the help." Lottie grabbed a body brush and a mane comb from a shelf nearby.

Peter grunted, which Lottie took as a

yes. She brushed and combed the horses until their coats gleamed. She had just gotten a bucket to rinse the brush in when she heard hooves drumming on the ground outside.

She went to see which horse was galloping so fast. But Peter appeared and shooed her back into the stable.

"It's Lady Slyden!" he hissed. "Don't come out or we'll both be in trouble!"

Lottie wanted to argue, but he seemed really anxious, so she didn't. She hid inside an empty stall and peeked through a narrow gap in the wooden boards.

"Quickly, boy! I haven't got all day!" said a high-pitched voice.

"Yes, My Lady," mumbled Peter.

There was a loud neighing.

"Lazy animal! It was far too slow," snapped Lady Slyden. "I'll take a different one for a ride tomorrow morning. It can be that large black horse over there."

Lottie caught a glimpse of Lady Slyden as she climbed off the horse. She had a haughty look in her eyes and her mouth sat in a straight line, as if she never smiled. She wore cream riding pants and a navy jacket, and had her hair twisted into a bun. She stared suspiciously at the stable for a moment and then stalked away, cracking her whip against the ground. Climbing into a large car, she drove off down a narrow lane.

Peter came back inside. "I don't like lending her horses. I know she whips them too hard when she gets angry." He shuddered. "But Queen Sofia lets her borrow them, so there's nothing I can do."

"That's horrible!" cried Lottie. "If I see her using the whip too much, I'll go and tell the queen right away."

A smile crept onto Peter's face. "You're not afraid of what anyone else thinks, are you?"

"I'm not scared of telling Queen Sofia what I see," said Lottie firmly. "Especially if it means I'm looking out for the horses."

"Well, thanks for helping me groom them," said Peter.

Lottie grinned. "It was really fun! Now I think the foal needs some fresh air."

Peter let her open the door of the stall where the mother and foal lay resting. The mare nuzzled the baby until she stood up on her wobbly little legs. The white star on her forehead showed clearly despite the dim light of the stable.

"Come on, Twinkle," said Lottie softly.

"I'm going across the fields to get some more hay," called Peter. "I'll be back in half an hour."

Lottie waved good-bye to Peter and watched the foal follow her mother out into the yard. Her little tail swished with excitement when she reached the grass. Then she galloped away, leaping around the meadow with her mane flying.

Lottie laughed and went over to pet her. The foal whinnied and tried to nibble her ear.

"So you're name is Twinkle," said Lottie. "You're very good at galloping for a foal that's only two weeks old."

Twinkle shook her mane and whinnied, as if she agreed with everything Lottie said.

As Lottie scratched between the foal's ears, a movement caught her eye. A lime-green hat appeared, bobbing along near the tulips. Queen Sofia was walking through the garden, leading a whole group of kings, queens, princes, and princesses.

Lottie froze. While she'd been grooming the horses, Queen Sofia's guests must have finished their dancing and come out for a walk. She couldn't be seen with hay on her dress and mud on her shoes. She'd get in lots of trouble.

The queen's voice drifted over. "These are the best tulips for miles around! Have a good look at them and then I'll take you to see my wonderful fountains."

Lottie began to run back to the stable to hide, when she noticed its gate. Her heart skipped a beat. The gate was wide open and swinging gently in the breeze. Had she left it like that? She didn't remember closing it after walking into the field. She frowned, angry at herself for being so forgetful.

Had any horses wandered out through it? She scanned the gardens. Two large horses stood by a fountain, bending their heads to drink from it. One was a dappled gray and the other was Honey, the sandy-colored horse. She had to get them back into the field quickly. Soon all the kings and queens would turn the corner and see what was happening. Queen Sofia would not be pleased to find horses trampling her flower beds.

Lottie dashed over to the fountain. Peter was still getting hay, so she would have to figure this out on her own.

"There's one more flower bed of tulips to show you," said Queen Sofia. "Do come this way."

Lottie looked up, her heart racing. But no one appeared. Phew! The queen must have taken them in a different direction. Hopefully that would give her more time to catch the horses.

She reached the dappled gray horse and patted his side, urging him down the path and back into the field. Quickly closing the gate, she headed toward Honey, who was trotting farther into the garden.

"Come back, Honey!" hissed Lottie, starting to chase her.

But Honey kept going.

Lottie heard footsteps and turned to find the princess with the dark curly hair and yellow dress running toward her.

"I've come to help you," panted the princess in yellow. "I'm Isabella. Don't worry; no one else has noticed that horse. They're all still looking at the tulips."

"Oh, good!" said Lottie. "It'll be much easier to catch her with your help. If you run one way and I run the other, then we can make her go back toward the gate. Ready?"

Isabella nodded.

They crept down the path, trying
to catch Honey. But the horse seemed to
understand their plan and trotted away
even faster, past a duck pond and a row
of trees covered in blossoms.

"Well, that didn't work!" said Lottie,
pausing to catch her breath.

"Maybe one of us should distract her,
while the other sneaks up behind her?"
said Isabella.

Lottie nodded; it sounded just like a
ninja move. "That's a great idea. You get
her attention and I'll sneak around."

Isabella started talking to Honey and
snapping her fingers. Honey pricked up
her ears and took a step closer.

Meanwhile, Lottie slipped to the side
of the horse, patting her on the rump
to make her walk forward. Finally, they
managed to coax her back down the
path. As they rounded the last corner,

the princess with the long black hair and turquoise dress was standing by the gate. She smiled and opened the gate to let Honey walk through.

The princess with short blonde hair stood there, too, watching with her hands on her hips. "For goodness' sake!" she said, rolling her eyes. "Don't you know you shouldn't let horses wander around Queen Sofia's garden?"

CHAPTER FIVE

Lottie's Secret

"Of course I know that Queen Sofia doesn't want horses in her garden!" said Lottie. "It was just an accident."

The princess with the blonde hair shrugged.

Lottie gave Honey one final pat and closed the gate behind her.

"Thanks for helping us," Isabella told the princess dressed in turquoise.

"That's OK!" she replied. "We slipped

away from the grown-ups when we saw
what you were doing."

Isabella smiled at her. "I'm Isabella, by
the way. I'm from Belatina, a kingdom of
tropical rain forests."

The princess in turquoise smiled back
shyly. "I'm Amina from Kamala, by the
Eastern Sea."

Lottie grinned. "And I'm Lottie from the
kingdom of Middingland."

The princess with blonde hair took
her hands off her hips and sighed. "I'm
Princess Rosalind, from Dalvia in the cold
North. We'd better get out of this mud
and join the others before Queen Sofia
notices we're missing."

"Just a minute," said Lottie. "I have
something to tell you. Actually, it's an
awesome princess secret and it will lead to
big adventures." She paused dramatically.

"Ooh, what is it?" asked Isabella.

The sound of voices grew louder. Queen Sofia was just around the corner.

"I can't tell you yet." Lottie fixed them with her green eyes and lowered her voice mysteriously. "People might hear us. But if you come and meet me at nine o'clock tomorrow morning under those trees, I'll explain it all." She pointed at the trees covered with blossoms.

"It had better not be boring," said Rosalind.

"It's not boring!" snapped Lottie.

"I'll come," said Isabella, pushing her dark curls over her shoulders.

"I will, too," said Amina.

"Oh, all right, then." Rosalind rolled her eyes. "I'll come, too."

"Great! It's going to be fantastic! You'll see," said Lottie.

Queen Sofia marched into view, followed by a crowd of kings and queens. Lottie quickly stepped behind Amina so that they wouldn't see the mud splatters and hay on her dress.

"Are you looking at the horses, girls?" asked the queen kindly. "There are lots of lovely horses in my stable. Some are very valuable because they're racehorses and they've won a lot of prizes. That little foal might become a racehorse one day, just like her mother was."

The princesses nodded and curtsied and then the group moved on.

Lottie beamed at Isabella, Amina, and Rosalind. These girls just might make perfect Rescue Princesses. Isabella seemed really friendly and Amina seemed nice, too. She wasn't quite so sure about Rosalind.

The girls hurried over to join the back of the group, which was now heading toward the fountains.

"Oops! Sorry!" cried Isabella as she tripped over a stone and knocked over three princes.

Lottie frowned. She hoped that the girls would be able to climb and run and balance. Her sister Emily's animal rescues had involved a lot of that kind of thing. Lottie was sure she could do it all (probably better than her sister). But what about the others? She crossed her fingers hopefully. Tomorrow she would find out what they could do.

Lottie woke up early the next morning, feeling full of energy. She took out the four magic rings, slipped the ruby one onto her finger, and put the others in her dress pocket. Somehow it just seemed right for the ruby ring to be hers. She really hoped that something special would happen today and the jewels would start working. What was the point of having magical rings if they didn't do anything?

Tiptoeing carefully, she went downstairs to the dining room and out through the glass doors into the garden. Little white clouds chased one another across the blue sky, and even the gray turrets on top of the palace looked bright and cheerful.

When she reached the blossom-covered trees, Lottie discovered that Amina and Rosalind were already waiting for her. Rosalind was wearing a short blue dress, and her blonde hair gleamed in the morning sunshine. Amina shifted from one foot to the other, her black hair swaying.

"Go ahead!" said Rosalind, not even

bothering to say hello. "Tell us this amazing *Big Secret*."

Lottie looked at her sharply. "Where's Isabella? I want to wait until everyone's here."

With the sound of hurrying footsteps, Isabella broke through the trees. "Sorry! Here I am!" she panted.

"I think we should go a little farther away," said Lottie. "Follow me." She led them past the duck pond and around the edge of the horses' paddock.

Twinkle the foal came galloping across the field and stuck her head over the fence right next to them.

"Hello, Twinkle," said Lottie, stroking her velvety nose.

Twinkle shook her head and whinnied a greeting.

"What a cute foal," said Amina. "She reminds me of my horse back home."

"She's very pretty with that white star on her forehead." Rosalind reached up to scratch between her ears.

Twinkle nibbled at Lottie's curly hair, making her giggle.

"She really likes you!" laughed Isabella.

Lottie saw Peter up at the stable yard and waved to him. "Let's keep going," she said. "We can always come and see Twinkle again on the way back."

They walked across the next field and into the narrow lane where Lady Slyden had driven her car the day before.

"Are we stopping soon? My feet hurt," said Rosalind.

"Let's go a little farther," said Lottie, leading them down the lane.

The fields on either side were full of sheep. Lambs frolicked across the grass, shaking their little woolly tails. The lane twisted and turned. Rounding a corner, the princesses found themselves by a stream with steep banks. Water tinkled along the stony riverbed.

Lottie stopped and turned to face the others. "OK, we're far enough away from the palace now. But I need to ask you all something really important before we start." She paused, looking at them. "Do you love animals?"

Isabella, Amina, and Rosalind nodded eagerly.

"My sister, Emily, started a secret club with her friends to rescue animals in trouble," said Lottie. "And when she went away to the Royal Academy for Princesses, she handed it over to me. It's Top Secret and for princesses only. No princes or grown-ups allowed!"

CHAPTER SIX

Rescue Princess Tryouts

"I love secret clubs!" said Isabella, her eyes sparkling. "It would be great to rescue animals without any grown-up help."

Lottie grinned. "We'll be called the Rescue Princesses! If you want to join, you have to show me what you can do."

"What do you mean?" asked Amina. "Will it be hard?"

"We'll be climbing trees and doing acrobatics and stuff like that. We'll do lots of training," said Lottie. "But for the tryouts we just need to find somewhere to test your skills."

"So what animals have you rescued so far?" asked Rosalind.

"Only a bumblebee!" Lottie frowned at her. "But I've only just started." She glanced over at the stream. "Look! We can use that log over there to balance on!"

The log bridged the gap between one side of the stream and the other. The banks were high and there was a long drop from the log down to the water.

"All you have to do is walk across and back again." Lottie walked confidently along the log, placing one foot in front of the other. Halfway across, she suddenly realized how far she would fall if she lost her balance. But she held her breath and kept walking.

"See? It's easy!" she told the others. "Now it's your turn."

Isabella, Rosalind, and Amina looked at her doubtfully.

"What if we fall off?" said Isabella. "My mom will be mad if I get wet."

"You'll be fine!" said Lottie impatiently. "Come on!"

"I'll try." Amina put one foot on the log. Then she skimmed lightly across it and back again.

"Fantastic!" cried Lottie, making Amina blush.

"All right!" said Isabella. "I'll try, too." But as soon as she began to walk, the log wobbled alarmingly. "Whoa!" she yelled, flapping her arms to try and keep her balance.

Amina pulled her back onto the bank again.

"Don't worry!" said Lottie, hiding her disappointment. "It was only your first time! At least you tried."

They all looked at Rosalind.

"I'm not sure I want to try out for your club yet," said Rosalind, folding her arms. "How do I know it will be fun?"

Lottie looked at her and frowned.

"We'll make it fun," said Isabella. "*And* we'll get to help animals."

"And training together will be really cool. It's not all about balancing. I know someone who can teach us ninja moves!" said Lottie, crossing back over the log to join the other princesses.

The others stared at her, wide-eyed.

"Ninja moves!" Rosalind's blue eyes glinted. "I would definitely like to learn some of those!"

"And we each get a Rescue Princess ring." Lottie pulled the rings out of her dress pocket. "My sister, Emily, and her friends used them. If you press the jewel in the center, it lights up and then we can send messages to each other." She held the rings out to show them.

"I want this one!" Rosalind grabbed the sapphire ring and pressed the jewel hard. "But it's not doing anything! Maybe your sister was making it up."

Lottie glared at her. "She wouldn't do that! I don't know why they're not turning on yet. But maybe we all have to be wearing them at the same time. Maybe that's how they work."

"I'd like this one, please." Isabella picked up the yellow topaz.

"Thank you, this is beautiful," said Amina, taking the emerald ring.

"And I've got the ruby one," said Lottie, showing them hers.

The princesses slid the rings onto their fingers and gazed at the sparkling jewels.

Rosalind pressed the sapphire again. "It still isn't working."

Lottie pressed her ruby, but nothing happened.

"Mine's not working, either." Isabella stared at her yellow topaz, and Amina also shook her head.

Lottie frowned. "I don't understand. They should be lighting up by now." She shook her head. What could be going wrong?

"Maybe you broke them on the way here," said Rosalind.

Lottie flushed angrily. But before she could reply, a thundering noise swept down the lane. The princesses looked around, unsure which way it was coming from. It grew louder. The ground began to shake.

"What's that?" called Isabella.

Amina turned pale.

"Come this way!" yelled Lottie, trying to get them to hide.

But before they had time to move, a huge dark shape burst around the corner and rushed toward them.

Rosalind let out a shriek, which made the dark shape rear up, and two massive hooves flailed in the air above them.

Lottie caught a glimpse of a figure with tall riding boots and cream riding pants, sitting on top of the giant animal.

"Don't worry!" she called to the others. "It's only a horse. It'll be all right." But her words were drowned out by a loud neighing and the cracking of a whip.

Isabella, Rosalind, and Amina started running up the lane toward the palace garden.

"Wait!" shouted Lottie, but the other princesses didn't even look back.

The black horse calmed down and shook his bridle restlessly.

"Silly girls!" snapped the rider in a haughty voice. "You shouldn't be sneaking around outside the palace. You nearly caused an accident."

Lottie jumped, recognizing the voice of Lady Slyden, the woman she'd seen at the stable yesterday.

"Don't stand there staring at me!" ordered Lady Slyden. "Go back to the palace like your silly friends." She glared at Lottie, cracked her whip, and sped away without waiting for a reply.

Lottie watched her go. Then she turned slowly and walked back toward the palace.

As she went past the paddock, Twinkle trotted along and put her head over the fence again. Lottie stroked the little foal's nose. But her heart felt heavy.

Not because of Lady Slyden's rudeness, she didn't care about that. She was disappointed that the other princesses had rushed off so quickly. As soon as they had seen danger, they had all run away.

CHAPTER SEVEN

The Princesses' Dance Routine

When Lottie reached the palace, lunch
was being served in the dining room. The
large glass doors of the room opened out
into the garden. Waiters brought around
platters of delicious pizza, followed by
apple pie and ice cream.

Lottie ate hers silently.

"Are you all right, Lottie?" Her mom
looked surprised to see her so quiet.

Lottie nodded. "Can I have some more
chocolate ice cream?"

"I suppose so!" Her mom laughed, passing some to her. "Oh, you're wearing Emily's ruby ring. It was nice of her to give it to you."

Lottie nodded again. The ruby ring just reminded her of everything that had gone wrong this morning. The jewels weren't working and the other girls didn't seem to understand what being a Rescue Princess was really about. But *she* was still determined to help animals in trouble, even if she had to do it on her own.

💜

After lunch, Queen Sofia divided all the kings, queens, princes, and princesses into groups to learn new dances. She gathered Lottie, Isabella, Amina, and Rosalind together.

"It would be wonderful if you four princesses would do a dance on the final day of the festival," she boomed. "Would you like to do that?"

The princesses nodded.

Queen Sofia glanced at a group of princes who were slouching in a corner. "Perhaps you could make up something that involves those princes, too. You could all hold hands as you dance. That would be nice!"

"No!" cried Lottie and Rosalind together.

"I mean, I don't think that's a very good idea, Your Majesty," Lottie added. She could see that Rosalind was just as horrified as she was at the queen's suggestion. The two girls exchanged a grin. Maybe Rosalind wasn't so bad after all, Lottie thought.

"I think the princes might want to dance by themselves," said Amina quietly.

"Very well, then!" Queen Sofia handed

them a CD player. "If you go along the hallway, you'll find a room that is suitable for practicing your dance. There's some music to choose from on the windowsill."

The girls curtsied and hurried away. At the end of the hallway, they found a large sitting room full of sofas and armchairs. Lottie set the CD player down on the windowsill and turned to face the other princesses. They were all still wearing their rings, she noticed.

"We're sorry we ran away before," Isabella told her. "Once we stopped running, we realized that it must have been a horse that suddenly came around the corner. But it was so huge and it galloped so fast!"

"That's all right," said Lottie, forgiving them instantly.

"We still want to join the Rescue Princesses," added Amina.

"Especially if you can get these rings to actually work," said Rosalind.

Lottie pressed the ruby in her ring again. "They are supposed to work. You'll just have to believe me."

"I believe you," said Isabella.

Lottie smiled back at her. "I suppose we'd better get started on this dance for Queen Sofia. What kind of dance should we do?"

"A tap dance!" cried Isabella.

"Hip-hop!" said Rosalind firmly.

"I like ballet," said Amina.

"Let's play some of this music and decide what we like the most." Lottie turned on the CD player and fiddled with the buttons.

The girls pushed the sofas and armchairs toward the walls to give themselves more room. Then they listened to several pieces of music, kicking off their shoes and trying out some dance moves.

"Actually, I really like this pop song!" Isabella wobbled around, nearly crashing into a bookcase.

"I do, too!" Lottie clapped her hands to the rhythm. "I listen to this at home."

Amina nodded. "Let's do our dance to this one, then."

"We could start with our arms together and then move them like this." Lottie showed them her dance move.

"Then we go: step together, step and turn." Isabella's face lit up as she danced.

The door opened, and Ally came in. "Hello, princesses! Queen Sofia sent me to see how you're doing. Do you need help with anything?"

"We're fine, thanks, Ally," said Lottie. "We're almost finished figuring out the dance routine."

"But we haven't decided what costumes or dance shoes to wear," said Rosalind.

"I think we should wear dresses that match."

"I don't think it matters that much if we wear different costumes," said Lottie.

"Well, I think it does!" Rosalind put her hands on her hips.

"It would be nice if our dresses were the same," said Amina, pushing back her long hair. "And we need our jazz shoes. We can't perform barefoot."

"Queen Sofia has a whole closetful of costumes upstairs," said Ally. "Why don't I go and see if there's anything in the right sizes? Then I'll collect your jazz shoes on the way back."

"Great idea!" said Isabella.

"Thanks, Ally," said Lottie.

Ally smiled and hurried away to look for the costumes.

"All right! Let's go back to the beginning and see how the dance looks so far." Lottie went over to the CD player and pressed the button to start the music. "I'll just open the window. It's getting really hot in here." She pulled up the window to let in the breeze.

"And one, two, three, and spin!" Isabella counted to herself as she practiced the dance moves.

Lottie leaned over the CD player, wondering why the music hadn't come back on. Had she pressed the wrong button? Just as she was about to try again, a high-pitched voice floated up through the open window.

"You shouldn't have come here! I told you — we meet at midnight!"

Lottie's ears pricked up. That was a very strange thing to say. Why would someone be meeting at midnight? She leaned forward, trying to see who was talking below.

"What are you doing?" asked Rosalind.

Lottie swung around and put a finger on her lips to signal the others to whisper.

Someone else spoke below them. It was a man's voice this time. "But, My Lady! I couldn't remember where I was supposed to park the van. So I had to come and see you."

"We've been through this over and over again! Park it by the stream on the corner of the lane, then walk up to the stable to help me," said the high-pitched voice.

With a sudden shiver, Lottie realized that she knew who it was. That voice belonged to Lady Slyden, the woman who'd been so rude to her that morning.

Leaning out a little farther, she could see that it was definitely Lady Slyden, still wearing her cream riding pants and with her hair twisted into a bun.

"What are we looking at?" whispered Isabella as she and Amina joined the other two girls at the window.

Lottie pointed at Lady Slyden and her servant standing in the garden below.

"How many horses are we taking?" said the man. "It's not a very big van, you know."

"Hush, fool! Are you trying to tell my plans to the whole palace?" snapped Lady Slyden. "You'll fit in as many horses as I tell you to. Now, go away! I don't want to see you again till midnight."

Lottie's head was buzzing. Why were they talking about putting horses into a van? And why were they doing it at midnight?

CHAPTER EIGHT

The Wicked Lady Slyden

The princesses held their breaths as they watched Lady Slyden disappear along the garden path.

"What was that all about?" said Rosalind at last. "Why are they meeting at midnight?"

"That was Lady Slyden, the woman riding the black horse this morning," said Lottie grimly. "And if she's moving horses around in the middle of the night, I think it sounds very suspicious."

Isabella's dark eyes widened. "You don't think she's trying to steal Queen Sofia's horses, do you?"

"The queen did say that she has some very valuable racehorses," said Amina. "They're probably worth a lot of money."

"Poor horses!" said Lottie. "Peter, the boy from the stables, says that Lady Slyden is mean to them. She whips them too hard when she gets angry."

The other girls looked shocked.

Lottie gazed through the open window at the horses' paddock just beyond the garden. There were lots of horses out in the field, including Twinkle, who was frolicking around and around in circles. Even from far away, Lottie could see how much the foal was enjoying the fresh air. Twinkle skipped around, only stopping to shake her mane and flick her tail.

Lottie lifted her chin and marched over to the door. "I'm going to tell Queen Sofia about this right now!"

"You can't!" gasped Amina. "What if she thinks you made it all up?"

"She has to know what Lady Slyden's up to," said Lottie. "The horses are in danger."

"Good! I'll come, too!" said Rosalind.

Lottie and Rosalind dashed down the hallway, with Isabella and Amina close behind them. They ran into the hall where the opening ceremony had taken place the day before. Queen Sofia was sitting on a large wooden throne, talking to a group of young princes.

"No one expects you to do a dance that's too difficult," she was saying to them. "Try practicing the hornpipe! All you have to do is fold your arms and hop on one leg."

Lottie felt a little less sure of herself now that she was right in front of the queen. She took a deep breath. "Your Majesty!" she called out. "We've got something really important to tell you!"

"It's about your horses," added Rosalind.

"Horses?" Queen Sofia looked at the princesses and shook her head, making her lime-green hat wobble. One of the young princes giggled, but she took no notice. Instead, she rose from her throne and towered over the girls.

"Princesses!" she said sternly. "Just look at yourselves! You should be walking and curtsying like proper young ladies. But instead you RAN in like PUPPIES. Your hair is a MESS and you have BARE FEET!"

There was silence. The princesses stared at their bare feet.

"But, Queen Sofia," began Lottie. "We

were just waiting for Ally to come back with our dance shoes and we heard —"

"Enough!" cried the queen. "I will not listen to anyone who comes in with bare feet."

The princesses slunk back out, not daring to speak until they reached the hallway.

"That was terrible!" cried Isabella. "What are we going to do?"

"What's the matter, princesses?" Ally hurried up to them, carrying lots of dance shoes and an armful of dresses.

"We think that Lady Slyden is planning to steal some of Queen Sofia's horses. We tried to tell the queen, but she wouldn't listen to us," said Lottie. She explained what they had overheard through the open window.

Ally's forehead creased with worry. "I don't trust Lady Slyden," she said at last.

"And I know she doesn't treat horses very well."

"Then we'll have to go to the stable at midnight and stop her," said Lottie.

The princesses looked at one another.

"But what if the kings and queens catch us sneaking out?" said Amina, her brown eyes wide. "Maybe we should try talking to Queen Sofia again."

"There's no point," said Rosalind. "She won't listen."

"Leaving the palace at midnight will be scary." Isabella looked solemn. "But we have to try for the sake of the horses."

"I can help you get away from here without anyone seeing you," said Ally. "But for now you'd better go and get changed. It's almost time for the banquet."

The princesses rushed back to their rooms to get changed. Lottie took a long red dress dotted with sequins out of her wardrobe. She put it on and added a golden crown decorated with rubies to match her ruby ring. Her green eyes sparkled back at her from the mirror.

Just then, the cuckoo clock on the wall chirped six o'clock. Lottie hurried out of her room and caught up with the others at the top of the stairs. Isabella turned and smiled as she saw Lottie coming. Her yellow dress floated out at the hem and a swirly gold tiara gleamed on top of her dark curls.

Rosalind and Amina had put on their best clothes, too. Rosalind wore a dark-blue dress, and her tiara was studded with the biggest emeralds that Lottie had ever seen. Amina's turquoise dress was tied in an elegant knot at one shoulder, and her tiara was made from arching loops of silver.

"We saw Lady Slyden," hissed Rosalind, pointing at the hallway below.

"She's talking to Queen Sofia," whispered Amina. "How can she act so friendly when she's planning to steal the queen's horses?" She leaned in for a closer look, her long black hair hanging over the banister.

"She's just pretending to be nice," said Lottie darkly. "I think we should keep an eye on her."

The princesses watched Lady Slyden throughout the first course of the banquet, which was soup with buttered rolls, and they watched her during the main course that followed. Lady Slyden rose from her seat and disappeared just as the sticky toffee pudding was served.

Lottie cast a worried look at the other princesses. Lady Slyden must be going to get ready for tonight.

"Mom? Can I go back to my room? I'm tired now," said Lottie.

The queen of Middingland raised her eyebrows. "And miss the sticky toffee pudding? Are you sure you're feeling all right, Lottie? You need to stay here and sit up straight. It's important for you to practice behaving nicely at banquets."

Lottie sighed and tapped her spoon on the table. How could sitting still at banquets be important when there were ninja moves to learn and horses to save?

CHAPTER NINE

Ninjas in the Palace

At last, the banquet ended. The princesses raced up to Lottie's room, where Ally showed them how to move around without being seen. Then they practiced tiptoeing stealthily up and down the hallway.

"I want to learn more ninja moves. This is so much fun!" cried Rosalind, flitting past like a shadow.

"I've heard that there's a book that contains every single ninja secret inside it," said Ally. "It's called *The Book of Ninja* and it's said to have been lost for a long time."

"I wish I could find it and read it," said Rosalind.

Isabella tripped over a wrinkle in the carpet and fell to her knees. "I don't think I'll ever be good at this!" she gasped.

"You're doing very well, Princess Isabella," said Ally. "Maybe a mug of hot chocolate would help."

Ally went downstairs and reappeared after a few minutes with a tray. The princesses sat on Lottie's bed to sip their mugs of hot chocolate. Lottie looked at the cuckoo clock on the wall. It was only eight thirty. There were still hours to go until midnight.

"I have a great idea!" exclaimed Amina, staring at the pile of dance costumes that Ally had left on Lottie's bed. She put down her mug and began sorting through the leotards and skirts. "These dance dresses that Ally found for us — if we wear a dark color tonight then no one will see us in the shadows." She pulled a shiny black dress out of the pile.

"Good idea! And we could put them on underneath our nightgowns when we go to bed," said Isabella.

"Here are some more of them." Lottie handed out the dresses so that they each had one. "You're right, Amina. This will make it much easier to reach the stables without anyone seeing us."

"But when we get there, how will we stop Lady Slyden from taking away the horses?" asked Rosalind.

Lottie thought for a moment. "I don't know," she said. "We might be able to distract her. We'll have to think quickly."

There was a knock at the door and the

princesses hid the black costumes behind their backs. The door opened and Lottie's mom came in.

"It's time for bed, all of you," said the queen of Middingland, smiling. "It will be a busy day tomorrow, full of excitement. So you need plenty of rest. Sleep well!"

"We will!" chorused the princesses.

When the queen closed the door again, they collapsed, laughing, on the bed.

"It will be a lovely night of rest, full of ninja action!" giggled Isabella.

At last, Lottie managed to stop laughing. "You'd better go before my mom comes back. Don't forget your black dresses. I'll meet you at the bottom of the stairs at ten to midnight."

Lottie lay in bed, staring at the clock. The minutes ticked by very slowly. Her eyelids began to close.

"Cuckoo!" The bird inside the wooden clock popped out and chirped eleven times.

Lottie sat straight up. She must have fallen asleep. Thank goodness for the cuckoo clock. She jumped out of bed and pulled off her nightgown to reveal the black dance dress underneath. There was less than an hour to wait now. Maybe she should get her flashlight ready.

She grabbed it from the bedside table and switched it on and off a few times under the covers. Then she took off her ruby ring and turned it over in her hand. If only the rings were working! She could send a message to the others. She tapped the ruby with her fingernail. But nothing happened. She rubbed it against her pillow. Still nothing.

She looked at the clock again. Half an hour to go. She frowned. It wasn't just the rings that were bothering her. What if Isabella tripped over something again? What if Amina got scared? Or what if Rosalind started arguing about everything? There were so many things that could go wrong.

Finally, at quarter to twelve, Lottie slipped on her shoes. Her bedroom door made a loud creak when it opened. But somehow she managed to close it quietly and creep down the hallway.

The palace was so silent that she hardly dared to breathe. She felt her way to the bottom of the stairs, not wanting to switch the flashlight on in case someone saw the light. Her heart thumped in the darkness. *This is for the horses*, she reminded herself. She couldn't let them get stolen by the horrible Lady Slyden.

Three more princess shadows slipped down the stairs to join her. The black dresses worked well, thought Lottie. The others were hard to spot in the dark.

"Is that you, Lottie?" murmured Isabella.

Lottie switched on her light. "Yes, it's me!" she whispered. "Are you ready?"

The others nodded.

Lottie flicked the light off again. The princesses tiptoed into the dining room and unlocked the doors that led outside. The garden was lit by a silver crescent moon that bobbed on a sea of clouds. Now they just had to cross the garden without being seen.

Remembering their ninja training, the princesses looked around for good places to hide. Then they ran across the lawn one by one, darting behind trees and statues. Lottie's red curls bounced as her feet flew over the damp grass. She joined the others by the gate

to the horses' field and tried to catch her breath.

She looked at her new friends, doubt creeping into her mind. Were they really going to be able to help the horses? Isabella had already tripped over a potted plant and Amina looked terrified.

"There's no sign of Lady Slyden or her servant yet," said Isabella, scanning the fields.

"Maybe they're already inside the stable." Amina's voice wobbled a little.

"They can't be. We'd be able to hear them," said Rosalind.

The princesses listened carefully. The trees rustled and an owl hooted a long way off.

"You're right, they can't be here yet," said Lottie. "Let's go around to the back of the stables. That way we'll be completely hidden before they arrive."

They crept across the stable yard. Isabella tripped over an animal's drinking trough, which made a loud clatter.

"Shh!" said Rosalind.

One horse put his head over his stall's door and snorted.

Lottie stopped suddenly. "Why aren't there more of them?" she asked.

"What do you mean?" said Amina nervously.

"There's only one horse looking out of the stable." Lottie pointed it out. "There should be more."

"Maybe the others are all asleep," said Rosalind.

Lottie went to look over each stall door. A cold dread rose inside her as she counted the empty stalls. There were five horses in the front stalls. She was sure there had been more than that yesterday.

She ran into the stable, checking the inside stalls one by one.

"Come back!" hissed Rosalind. "They'll see us if we hide in there."

Lottie ignored her. With a racing heart, she peered into Twinkle's stall and flicked on her flashlight. The foal's mother was standing up, tossing her mane anxiously. But the little foal was gone.

Somewhere in the distance, a clock chimed midnight.

The other princesses ran into the stable to join Lottie. Rosalind grabbed the flashlight and shone it all around.

"What is it, Lottie?" cried Isabella. "You look awful!"

Lottie blinked back her tears. "We're too late! Lady Slyden's already been here — and she's taken Twinkle."

CHAPTER TEN

Finding Twinkle

"We have to go and tell Queen Sofia what's happened," gasped Amina.

"We can't! If we go back to the palace now, it gives Lady Slyden more time to get away!" said Lottie. "Anyway, how can we wake up the queen in the middle of the night?"

There was a moment of silence. No one liked the idea of waking up Queen Sofia.

"We could try to follow Lady Slyden and

the horses," said Isabella. "Do you think we'd catch up with them?"

Lottie's green eyes flashed. "I'm going to try. Who's coming with me?"

"I am," said Amina quickly. "I can't believe they took a little foal away from its mother. They should be ashamed of themselves."

"I'm coming, too," Isabella said firmly.

Rosalind put her hands on her hips. "Well, I'm not letting all of you have an adventure without me!"

Lottie grinned and held out her hand. "Then we're Rescue Princesses together!"

Isabella, Amina, and Rosalind placed their hands on Lottie's, one on top of the other. The heart-shaped jewels in their rings lit up with a sudden glow that lasted for a few seconds and then went out.

"Awesome!" cried Isabella, staring at the jewels.

"We finally made them work," Rosalind said softly.

"Now we're really Rescue Princesses!" said Lottie, her eyes sparkling. "Come on, let's go! We've got to catch up with Lady Slyden!"

The circle of light from Lottie's flashlight led the way as they raced across the field. They slowed down as they reached the narrow lane.

"We don't know where they are," said Rosalind. "We could be going in the wrong direction."

"Lady Slyden told her servant to park his van by the stream," Lottie reminded her. "So I think they must be this way."

They sneaked down the lane until Lottie stopped them. She held a finger up to her lips.

They could hear voices.

They crept closer and hid next to the wall on one side of the lane. A few yards away, a man struggled with a tall stallion that had reared up on its hind legs. He was pulling it toward a black van.

"The horse doesn't want to go into the van," whispered Amina.

"Get in there now or I'll get my whip out!" hissed Lady Slyden.

"How dare she?" whispered Lottie furiously. "I wish Queen Sofia could see this!"

The man finally managed to pull the horse into the van.

"That's the last one, My Lady," he said, climbing out of the van and closing the door.

"Good!" said Lady Slyden. "Get out the map and I'll show you where you're going. You have to get there as fast as you can."

"But, My Lady! I can't drive too fast in case it upsets the horses."

"You will do as I say!" snapped Lady Slyden.

The servant and Lady Slyden walked to the front of the van and bent over a large map.

The princesses exchanged looks. This was their chance! They tiptoed across the lane toward the stream. When they were sure that no one was looking, they dashed out of the shadows and hid behind the van.

Rosalind shaded her eyes to look through the little window in the van door. "The poor horses are really squashed in there."

"Let's get them out," whispered Amina.

Lottie pulled gently on the handle, opening the door without a sound. There were four fully grown horses inside and

Twinkle, the little foal. The animals looked at the princesses with big dark eyes. Twinkle began to shiver.

"Poor things! They're really scared," said Amina.

"What should we do? If we get the horses out, Lady Slyden will hear the sound of their hooves on the road," said Isabella.

"I know! I'll use my new ninja moves," said Rosalind. "I'll sneak farther down the lane and do something to get their attention."

"Please be careful!" said Amina.

Rosalind flitted away into the darkness. Lottie peered around the side of the van. Lady Slyden and the man were still leaning over the map.

Then, out of the darkness came a very loud clanging, like someone hitting a tin can with a stick. Lady Slyden's head jerked up. She left the map at once and crept down the road toward the noise. Her servant followed her.

"I hope Rosalind knows what she's doing," said Isabella with a shiver.

"Now's our chance!" hissed Lottie. "Quickly! We've got to get these horses to safety."

CHAPTER ELEVEN

The Way Home

The three princesses climbed inside the van and untied the horses one by one. Then they led them carefully out and around the corner of the lane. Lottie guided Twinkle, talking soothingly to her and stroking her velvety coat. Twinkle stopped shivering and nibbled at Lottie's hair.

"The problem is that they'll know something's wrong as soon as they drive away," said Amina worriedly. "The van won't feel as heavy as it should."

Lottie bit her lip. "We need to put something heavy inside." She looked around and noticed some large rocks lying in the moonlit stream.

"I'll get those stones! They'll make it feel heavier." She quickly climbed down the bank and pulled one large rock out of the stream. She passed it up to Amina, who loaded it into the van.

She grabbed another rock. Her feet were wet and her hands were freezing, but she didn't care. The only thing that mattered was rescuing the horses.

Together, the girls loaded five large rocks into the van. Then they shut the door and rushed back around the corner to the horses just as Lady Slyden returned.

"Hurry up, you fool!" Lady Slyden told the man. "We don't know who else is out here. Do you *want* to be caught?"

The two figures dived into the van and drove away at top speed.

A shadow slipped along the lane and Rosalind appeared in front of them, grinning.

"They couldn't figure out what the noise was and then they got spooked," she said.

One of the horses let out a loud chuckling whinny, sending the girls into fits of laughter.

Lottie and Twinkle led the group of princesses and horses up the lane and through the fields. When she reached her own paddock, Twinkle galloped around, swishing her tail.

"You're happy to be home, aren't you, Twinkle?" laughed Lottie.

They were met at the stable by Peter, who was waving a flashlight around and looking frantic.

"What happened?" he asked. "I came down here to check on the horses and some of them were missing."

"Lady Slyden tried to steal them," said Lottie. "Even poor Twinkle."

Peter pointed his flashlight at the animals. "She chose all the young racehorses," he said angrily. "She probably wanted to sell them to make lots of money."

"I remember Queen Sofia saying that Twinkle might be a racehorse, too, one day," said Isabella.

"I can see why." Lottie grinned as Twinkle galloped past with her mane flying.

Peter began settling the horses back into their stalls. Lottie managed to catch Twinkle and lead her back. Twinkle's mother whinnied and nuzzled her little foal, and then they snuggled down

together on the hay. Twinkle closed her eyes and laid her head down. The white star on her forehead gleamed in the moonlight.

"I'm so glad you're safe again after such a scary night," Lottie told the little foal.

She stroked her soft ears one more time and then shut the stall door.

"I'll just get the horses some extra feed," said Peter, hurrying out of the stables.

Lottie noticed that the other princesses were all helping with the horses, too. Rosalind was smiling widely, Amina had stopped looking nervous, and Isabella hadn't tripped over anything. Something wonderful had happened to them all, ever since their rings had glowed.

Lottie looked down at her glistening ruby. *Jewels with special powers*, Emily had called them. She pressed the red stone and it blazed with light. "Calling all Rescue Princesses!" she whispered into it.

The jewels on the other girls' rings lit up, too. The sapphire, the emerald, and the yellow topaz all glowed brightly.

"Wow!" cried Amina.

The princesses crowded together to look at one another's glowing rings.

"Your voice sounded really clear just now," said Rosalind. "And it came right out of my ring."

"Mine, too," said Isabella.

"They're working perfectly," said Lottie, grinning. "We pulled off a great rescue tonight. It's almost as if these rings made us magical, too."

"I don't think our rescue was magic," said Isabella. "I think it was teamwork. Maybe the rings couldn't work the right way until *we* started working together."

Lottie smiled at her. "Maybe you're right!"

The sky began to lighten as the sun rose.

Peter came back in with a wheelbarrow full of hay. He stopped and looked at the princesses. "I just noticed how funny you all look," he said. "What are you wearing?"

"These are our black dancing dresses," Rosalind told him. "Very handy for sneaking across the palace garden at night!"

Peter looked a little confused. "I guess wearing black does camouflage you in the dark."

"Exactly!" said Isabella. "And now we'd better go. The grown-ups will wake up soon."

"Thanks for bringing the horses back to me," said Peter. "You're not really ordinary princesses, are you?"

"Not really!" laughed Lottie.

The princesses grinned at him. Then they linked their arms together and hurried back across the field toward the palace.

CHAPTER TWELVE

The Final Performance

Ally brought the princesses a delicious breakfast of warm rolls and honey, with tall glasses of strawberry milk. The girls sat at a table in Lottie's room and gobbled down their food. All the excitement and ninja moves of the night before had made them extremely hungry.

"Is it the last performance of the Dance Festival today?" asked Isabella, helping herself to another roll.

"Yes it is! And we still need to figure out our costumes," said Amina.

Rosalind brushed the crumbs off her hands and rummaged through the pile of dance dresses on Lottie's bed. She grinned at the others. "How about this?" She pulled a lime-green leotard out of the pile and held it up to show them.

"No way!" laughed Isabella. "That reminds me of Queen Sofia's hat."

Finally they agreed on golden dance dresses with black jazz shoes. After breakfast, they changed into the costumes and brushed their hair. Then they walked downstairs to the hall, where the final performance would take place.

Rows of chairs had been set up for the audience. The seats were already filling up with kings, queens, and other royalty. Everyone had put on their most splendid robes and dresses, and crowns and tiaras sparkled everywhere.

The princesses paused in the doorway, suddenly nervous about all the pairs of eyes that would be watching their dance routine.

"Queen Sofia?" A king in a blue turban bowed low. "Would you like me to find Lady Slyden and tell her we're ready to begin? She seems to be missing again."

Queen Sofia turned around, her lime-green hat quivering. "There's no need," she said firmly. "I found out some shocking news from my stableboy this morning. Lady Slyden has been unkind to the horses I lent her, and last night she tried to steal some of them. I've sent her a message telling her never to return to my palace, and she's lucky that I haven't had her arrested. How dare she behave so cruelly to my animals?"

The princesses beamed at one another.

"Peter must have told Queen Sofia all about Lady Slyden," whispered Lottie. "Good for him!"

"Good morning, princesses!" boomed Queen Sofia, seeing them standing together. "I'd like you to begin the grand performance. What kind of dance have you chosen?"

"Hip-hop," chorused the princesses.

"Hip-hop?" repeated Queen Sofia. "Excellent! I am quite in the mood for a little boogie."

Hiding their giggles, the princesses took up their starting positions. The hall fell silent. Then the beat of the song began. The princesses remembered all their dance moves perfectly. At the end, the audience clapped and cheered, and the girls dropped graceful curtsies.

Their act was followed by tap dances, ballet dances, and the princes' hornpipe. After the grand performance had finished, Lottie looked over at the door in the corner that led into the garden. She beckoned to the others and, while the grown-ups were still chatting, they slipped out of the door and raced across the lawn.

Lottie reached the gate first and climbed over it into the field.

"I wonder if the horses are tired after their adventure last night," said Amina.

Just then, Twinkle came trotting out of the stable. She whinnied excitedly when she saw them and galloped around and around in circles.

"Stop, Twinkle! You're making me dizzy," laughed Rosalind.

Twinkle stopped galloping and nibbled Lottie's hair.

"I think Twinkle's trying to say thank you," said Amina.

"You're welcome, Twinkle." Lottie rubbed the little foal's velvety nose. "Now I can't wait for our next rescue!"

"And we could find out more about the lost *Book of Ninja* that Ally talked about," suggested Rosalind.

"Whatever we do, we'll do it together." Isabella held out her hand with its special ring.

"Together!" said the others, putting their hands on top of hers.

The jewels in their rings lit up for a moment, making the girls catch their breath.

Twinkle whinnied and lifted up her front leg, too.

"You're joining in, Twinkle!" Lottie hugged her. "You really are the best foal in the world!"

Can't wait for
the Rescue Princesses' next
daring animal adventure?

The Lost Gold

Turn the page for
a sneak peek!

CHAPTER ONE

The Blue Butterfly

Princess Isabella crept through the rain forest with a small monkey riding on her shoulder. Parrots squawked to one another in the treetops and water drops from the last rain shower glinted on the broad leaves.

Suddenly, she froze. A sharp banging shattered the peace of the forest, and the tree trunk trembled under her fingers.

After a few moments, the banging happened again. It was louder this time and was followed by a high-pitched grinding sound that made Isabella shudder. Petro leapt back onto her shoulder and put his hands over his ears.

She hurried toward the sound, searching for what it could be. At last she saw something through the trees. There was a group of men standing in the middle of a clearing.

Isabella frowned. What were they doing? Where had the clearing come from? She was sure there had been thick forest here before.

One of the men began to use a metal saw to cut a tree. The grinding noise grew louder as the saw bit into the trunk. The tree started to sway and, very slowly, it toppled over and crashed to the ground.